BIONICLE®

Dark Destiny

by Greg Farshtey

SCHOLASTIC INC.
New York Toronto London Auckland Sydney
Mexico City New Delhi Hong Kong Buenos Aires

For Doug and Claudia

No part of this publication may be reproduced in whole or part, stored in a retrieval system, or transmitted in any form or by any means, electronic, mechanical, photocopying, recording, or otherwise, without written permission of the publisher. For information regarding permission, write to Scholastic Inc., Attention: Permissions Department, 557 Broadway, New York, NY 10012.

ISBN: 0-439-78795-5

12 11 10 9 8 7 6 5 4 3 2   6 7 8 9 10/0

Printed in the U.S.A.
First printing, April 2006

Characters

Island of Metru Nui

THE TURAGA

Dume	Elder of Metru Nui
Nuju	
Vakama	
Nokama	Former Toa Metru and Turaga of the villages of the
Onewa	island of Mata Nui
Whenua	
Matau	

THE MATORAN

Jaller	A Ta-Matoran villager, now serving as captain of the Ta-Metru Guard
Matoro	Ko-Matoran aide to Turaga Nuju
Hahli	Ga-Matoran Chronicler
Nuparu	Onu-Matoran engineer
Hewkii	Po-Matoran carver
Kongu	Le-Matoran Gukko rider

THE TOA

Takanuva	Toa of Light
Tahu Nuva	Toa Nuva of Fire
Gali Nuva	Toa Nuva of Water
Pohatu Nuva	Toa Nuva of Stone
Onua Nuva	Toa Nuva of Earth
Lewa Nuva	Toa Nuva of Air
Kopaka Nuva	Toa Nuva of Ice

Island of Voya Nui

THE MATORAN

Garan	Onu-Matoran leader of the resistance
Balta	Ta-Matoran, able to improvise tools from anything lying around
Kazi	Ko-Matoran with many secrets
Velika	Po-Matoran inventor
Dalu	Ga-Matoran fighter
Piruk	Le-Matoran, skilled in stealth

THE PIRAKA

Zaktan	Emerald-armored leader of the Piraka
Hakann	Crimson-armored Piraka
Reidak	Ebon-armored Piraka
Avak	Tan-armored Piraka
Thok	White-armored Piraka

INTRODUCTION

Turaga Dume, elder of Metru Nui, slammed shut the door of his chamber. Although his face was covered by a Kanohi mask, no one needed to see his expression to know he was filled with cold fury. He looked at the six Turaga assembled around the table, then made a sound of disgust and turned away.

"We have reached the end," he said, staring out the window at the city he loved. "In a matter of weeks — perhaps months — the Great Spirit Mata Nui will be dead. When he dies, so, too, will our universe. It is time to lower our voices, avert our eyes, and wait for the darkness."

He turned abruptly and pointed a shaking finger at the other Turaga. "But one of you . . .

could not let our tale conclude with dignity. One of you has betrayed us!"

Stunned by the accusation, the six Turaga looked at each other. Since their return to Metru Nui, they had spent almost all of their time in this chamber, trying to think of some way to forestall disaster. Turaga Dume and Turaga Nuju had read in the stars that Mata Nui was not merely asleep, as they had long believed, but was actually dying. Only the legendary Kanohi Mask of Life could save him.

In desperation, the Turaga sent the heroic Toa Nuva on a quest to the island of Voya Nui. Their mission was to find the Mask of Life and save the Great Spirit. Many days had passed with no word and no sign of them, until even Turaga Vakama conceded that they must have failed . . . or worse. Only the Toa of Light remained in the city, and there had been much debate about sending him to rescue the others. But it was agreed that a single Toa, even one as powerful as he, would stand no chance if six Toa Nuva had fallen. More, Dume insisted that if by some miracle the

Toa Nuva did return with the mask, Takanuva's presence in the city would be of vital importance.

That left the Turaga with nothing to do but wait and hope. As one day turned into the next, it became increasingly obvious that it was all in vain. The Toa Nuva were gone, the Great Spirit was doomed, and all he had created would perish with him.

"We had agreed that the Matoran would not be told," Dume continued. "After their great efforts to return to their homeland, it would be beyond cruelty to tell them their time would be cut short. So now I must ask — who among you dared to break this agreement? Who told the Matoran their world is about to die?"

"Now, wait," said Onewa, Turaga of Stone. "How do you even know anything was revealed? I hear no shouting in the streets, no wailing that the end is coming. Believe me, in my time, I have come to know the sounds of panic, and there are none to be heard."

Dume sat down heavily in his chair, as if the weight of all his years was on his shoulders. "Jaller is gone," he replied. "Jaller, who insisted so strongly that the Matoran had to know where the Toa Nuva had gone, and why. And with him are Matoro, Nuparu, Kongu, Hewkii, and Hahli, all of them vanished from their homes overnight. They were last seen in Le-Metru, heading for the abandoned underwater chutes that lead to the south."

"You don't mean . . . ?" began Whenua.

"Jaller would never be so foolish," said Vakama.

"Oh no," whispered Nokama, looking stricken. "I never thought he would . . ."

Dume turned to look at her. When he spoke, his voice was hard. "So. You told Jaller."

"Yes," Nokama replied, with more than a hint of defiance in her voice. "We are facing the possible end of the universe. The Matoran — our friends — have a right to know why they are going to die. But I never imagined Jaller would try to act on what I had shared with him."

Nuju whistled sharply twice, and then made a slashing motion across his throat. Vakama nodded in agreement. "You're right, Nuju. They will never make it to Voya Nui alive. We have no choice. We will have to send Takanuva to bring them back."

"Something I would gladly do," Dume replied. "Except that he's gone, too."

"You shouldn't have come," said Jaller.

"You shouldn't have gone," Takanuva answered.

The two of them were scouting ahead, while the other five Matoran moved cautiously across the blasted landscape. They had emerged from the underwater chutes only a few minutes before to find themselves on a long, narrow land bridge. They had no clear idea how to reach their destination, other than to travel south and then "up."

"Hahli was right," Jaller muttered. "It would have been easier to return to Mata Nui and sail south from there."

"It's a big ocean," said the Toa of Light.

"We still might never have found it. I'm not sure what one Toa and six Matoran will be able to do against whatever stopped the Toa Nuva, anyway."

"Whatever it is, we'll do it. But you should turn back. If anything happens to you, the city will be defenseless."

Takanuva gave a bitter chuckle. "And if Mata Nui dies, the city won't matter. Besides, I couldn't let you have all this fun by yourselves."

Jaller paused on a rise. In the distance he could see a tunnel mouth, and beyond that . . . what? There was no way to know. The Toa Nuva had traveled to Voya Nui in protective canisters, for the Turaga had said any other means of travel would be too dangerous. That meant the Matoran could not count on any opposition ahead having already been dealt with, for the Toa had not passed this way.

"Do you remember that time I went to Le-Wahi, and you had to come find me?" Takanuva asked, recalling when he had been a Matoran. "You know, in the cave."

"The cave full of stone rats," Jaller said, nodding. "You were about to be dessert."

"You charged in, grabbed me . . . we both fell down a hole . . . ended up in a venomous rockworm nest," said Takanuva, smiling. "Had to dig our way through a tunnel full of the remains of its meals to make it back to the surface. What a nightmare."

"I remember," said Jaller. "What made you think of that?"

"Just that I have a feeling that trip is going to seem like a Naming Day celebration compared to this one," answered the Toa of Light. "Go back, Jaller. Let me find the Toa Nuva and the Mask of Life. It's my job."

Jaller shook his head. "We all live in this universe. That means saving it is everyone's job."

Takanuva sighed. It was next to impossible to win an argument with Jaller, especially when he was right. Rather than continue the debate, the Toa of Light pointed up ahead. "At least let me scout the tunnel alone. If there is anything in there, I'm better equipped to deal with it."

"Be careful," said Jaller.

Takanuva laughed. "Now where's the fun in that?"

The six Matoran stood on the plateau, watching as Takanuva prepared to enter the tunnel. He had done a brief test of his elemental and mask powers, abilities he was still not completely used to. Once he felt ready, he surrounded his body with a luminescent glow and headed for the entrance.

Jaller watched as his friend took one step into the tunnel and utterly vanished. He blinked and looked again, for it made no sense. The Toa of Light's aura should have been able to pierce any darkness, making him visible until he was well inside the tunnel. Jaller could only think of one thing to say about this turn of events.

"Uh-oh."

In his previous life, as a Matoran, Takanuva had journeyed all over the island of Mata Nui. He had plunged into the frigid depths of the sea and climbed the snowy peak of Mount Ihu. He knew how it felt to be blasted with frigid air in the snowfields of Ko-Wahi. But he had never experienced true cold before, not like this.

His aura had vanished the instant he entered the tunnel. His efforts to restore it had failed, along with every other attempt to use his powers. He had stood up to Makuta, the master of shadows, and won, yet this darkness was proof against anything the Toa of Light could throw against it. Worse, it felt like he was surrounded by a mountain of ice, almost as though the warmth was being drained right out of his body.

He turned around, thinking it best to head back out again. But with the darkness so thick, he couldn't be sure he was facing the entrance anymore. If he went the wrong way, he might be lost forever.

Takanuva digested that cheerful thought. Then he called upon the Mask of Light again, reasoning that maybe a pinpoint beam of light might succeed where a wider glow had failed. His spirit soared when he actually saw the laser shoot forth. But a second later, it, too, had been consumed by the darkness.

Consumed . . .

Yes, that was what it felt like. It wasn't that his powers were failing. Something in this tunnel was devouring his light, something hidden and powerful . . . and very hungry.

Takanuva shuddered, but this time it wasn't from the cold.

# ONE

Garan sat on a rock and wondered how everything had managed to go so wrong. For a thousand years, he and other Matoran had eked out an existence on the island of Voya Nui. It wasn't easy, not with frequent volcanic eruptions, a dwindling water supply, no Turaga to lead them, and no Toa to protect them. Still, they somehow managed to thrive on this rocky island.

Then, mere weeks ago, it seemed as if their lives were about to change for the better. Six canisters washed up on the icy shore of the island. The powerful figures who emerged from them stated that they were Toa, come to guide the Matoran to a more secure future. Although, in some respects, they did not look like Toa — none of them wore Kanohi masks, for example — most Matoran were so thrilled by the newcomers' arrival that acceptance was easy.

From the start, the behavior of these new "Toa" was strange. They did little to improve the daily lives of the Matoran. They committed acts of what could best be called casual cruelty. When they did finally put the Matoran to work on major tasks, they were bizarre ones. Some Matoran were detailed to build a vast stronghold, one which they would never be allowed to enter. Others were set to work digging holes in the side of the volcano and carving vast trenches to collect the lava that spilled out.

It wasn't until later that Garan and a small group of his friends discovered the truth. These Toa were in fact raiders called Piraka, who had come to the island in search of some treasure they believed was hidden in the volcano. Worse, they were storing some sort of virus in their stronghold, one powerful enough to completely enslave a Matoran.

Before Garan's group could act on what they had learned, the Piraka struck. When they were done, virtually the entire Matoran population of Voya Nui had been made into slaves. In a desperate maneuver, Garan's best friend, Balta, got close enough to steal one of the virus launchers and bring it back to the others. Then he had vanished into the mountains, trying to lead away the Piraka who pursued him.

For the hundredth time in the past hour, Garan climbed up on an overhanging rock and scanned the mountainside for Balta. Lightning flashes illuminated the area for a kio around, but of his friend, there was no sign.

If they caught him, he's as good as dead, he told himself. *Or worse, he's become one of their mindless workers, laboring amidst the lava. No — I'll die myself before I'll let that be his fate.*

"Still no sign?"

Garan turned to see Dalu approaching. She had already asked three times to be allowed to search for Balta. Garan had said no, fearing that if the Piraka were nearby, she would be lost as well.

"No."

"Then I'm going," she said firmly. "He's out there and I'll find him."

"And if he's dead?"

"Then I'll avenge him," said Dalu.

Piruk scrambled up the slope, out of breath. He had to take a few gulps of air before he could get his message out. "I saw them — the Piraka! Hakann was in the lead, and he was carrying someone up to the volcano crater. I think he is going to throw someone into the lava!"

Garan glanced at Dalu. They were both thinking the same thing: Balta must have been captured and the Piraka were executing him. "Get the others!" Garan shouted at Piruk. "We leave now!"

The Piraka known as Reidak grunted under his burden. While the others had to carry only one Toa apiece, he was stuck with two, the Toa of Fire and the Toa of Water. It wasn't the first time he had been used as a pack hauler for the group, but that didn't make him any happier about it.

"Where's Zaktan?" he growled, looking around for the Piraka leader. "How come he doesn't have to carry one of these guys up the mountain?"

"That's simple," said Hakann. "Because he has us to do it."

"He took the masks and weapons we collected from these Toa back to the stronghold," said Avak, "leaving us to throw out the trash."

Hakann chuckled. These six Toa had appeared on Voya Nui and wound up on the losing end of a battle with the Piraka. Some of the victors had wanted to take the Toa prisoner and find out why they had come to this Mata Nui — forsaken hunk of rock. Did they know about the powerful Kanohi mask said to be hidden here? Were they out to get it for themselves, or had something else brought them to this volcanic isle?

Zaktan made it clear he didn't care. Even minus their masks and weapons, Toa were too much potential trouble. He ordered that they be tossed into the volcano and left to burn. Then he took the loot and departed.

Hakann glanced over his shoulder at the semiconscious Toa of Ice he carried. He had briefly considered approaching one of these Toa about an alliance of convenience against Zaktan. Then he decided that Toa, as a group, were too simplemindedly noble to ever consider such a thing. Zaktan was right about one thing — it *did* make more sense to kill the lot of them.

"How much farther?" snapped Vezok. "This Toa of Earth isn't getting any lighter."

"Then you shouldn't have hit him so hard," replied Hakann. "Just think — a little while ago, he was an all-powerful hero who could make . . . well, dirt do his bidding. Now he's just a heavily armored load for Vezok to carry and dump."

"Keep talking," replied Vezok. "You'll be following him into the lava."

"I don't think so," Hakann shot back. "I doubt I would look good charred black."

Avak suddenly stopped and dumped Pohatu Nuva on the ground. "I'm taking a rest. Whether he goes into the fire now or two minutes from now, he's just as dead."

"Why delay?" said Hakann, continuing up the slope. "I haven't gotten to kill a Toa in weeks. I say we throw them all in at once and see which one hits first."

Tahu Nuva's eyes flickered open. The first thing he noticed was that the ground was moving beneath him, but he was not walking. Then he realized both that his body felt strangely weak, and the reason for that — his Kanohi mask was gone. He glanced around for it, trying to conceal the fact that he was awake, but saw no sign.

It all came back to him. The Piraka . . . the sword fight . . . defeat. With their masks, the Toa Nuva had been unable to defeat these new enemies. What chance did they have without them?

He took a chance and lifted his head just enough to see where they were going. Up ahead, plumes of white smoke were rising from the crater of the volcano. It didn't take a genius to figure out their ultimate destination. The only way out he saw was to unleash whatever he could of his elemental power against Reidak, and hope it was enough to down the Piraka. Then he could rally the other Toa and they could make their escape.

Even as he conceived the plan, he realized it was doomed. But he wasn't going to go to his death being carried like a wounded Rahi. Better to go down fighting.

Tahu readied himself for the attack. That was when he noticed his hands were shaking. It took a moment for him to realize it wasn't just his hands, but his whole body, and Reidak, and in fact the entire mountainside.

"What's going on?" Reidak yelled.

"If there were a brain inside that thick armored skull of yours, you would know," Hakann answered, throwing Kopaka Nuva aside. "The volcano is erupting!"

As if on command, the mountaintop exploded, raining rock and magma and ash down upon them. The Piraka dropped their captives and scattered, trying to outrace the lava flow. Tahu instinctively tried to throw up a shield to protect himself and the others, before remembering he had no Mask of Shielding anymore.

"Pohatu!" he shouted. "We need you!"

The Toa Nuva of Stone was still trying to clear his head. The first thing he saw when his vision cleared was a wave of lava heading for a still-stunned Gali Nuva. There wasn't time to worry about where his Mask of Speed had gone, only to act. Summoning what elemental power he could, he raised a wall of stone to block the molten flow.

Seizing the chance, Lewa dashed over, grabbed Gali, and dragged her away even as the stone wall began to melt. "We need a bigger barricade!" he yelled.

"I can't!" said Pohatu, helping Onua to his feet. "Without the mask, my power is too weak."

"Then make . . . small ones," the Toa of Earth muttered. "Lots of them."

The six Toa Nuva staggered, stumbled, and ran across the mountainside as the lava flowed inexorably toward them. All along the way, Pohatu used his waning power to throw up stone barriers to check the magma's progress. They didn't work for long, and when they melted, the lava surged forward. Kopaka got caught in one such surge and badly burned his right leg. Had Tahu not been close by to help him, he would have fallen and been incinerated by the molten mass.

The Toa Nuva kept going long after they were clear of the volcano, heading northeast. Finally, Tahu climbed on a boulder that afforded him a good view of the ground they had covered. Seeing no sign of the Piraka, he signaled the others to rest.

"If we're fortunate, they'll think we're dead," the Toa Nuva of Fire said. "If not, they will be hunting us soon."

"Good," Kopaka answered. He was using his ice power to soothe the damage done to his muscle tissue, but nothing could hide the scorch marks on his armor. "I owe them for some pain. I intend to pay them back in kind."

"Who are they?" asked Gali.

"I don't know," answered Tahu. "But until we know otherwise, we have to assume they are here for the same thing we are: the Kanohi Mask of Life. And if they get it first, we can forget about saving the life of the Great Spirit. Mata Nui will die and the universe will go with him. We need our masks, we need our weapons . . . then we will settle our score with the Piraka."

From his perch atop a rocky ledge, Lewa broke in. "Visitors, coming from the north. Six Matoran."

"We can use them," said Gali. "They know this island, and we don't. They might even know where our masks would have been hidden. It looks like we will need any help we can get to achieve this mission."

"Achieve it, sister?" commented Kopaka. "I would say we need help just to survive it."

Dalu spotted the Toa Nuva first. "Strangers," she said. "There, in those rocks ahead. Not Matoran . . . not Piraka. Toa, maybe?"

A rumble of thunder rolled through the sky, followed by bright flashes of lightning. The storm had been building in intensity for days. Clouds blotted out the sun and the stars, all save one. For some unexplained reason, a lone red star managed to shine even through the thickest, blackest of storm clouds. Even more bizarre, the Onu-Matoran could have sworn the lightning was actually coming from the star itself.

"What do you think, Velika?" Garan asked, turning to the Po-Matoran.

"It is said that there was once a Rahi who looked up at the stars and believed them to be food belonging to a larger creature," Velika answered softly. "Each night, he would climb the tallest mountain and jump as high as he could, hoping to snatch a star for himself. Finally, he decided it could not be done, and more, that they were not food at all."

"Is there a point, and can you get to it?" grumbled Kazi. The Ko-Matoran had long ago lost patience with Velika's anecdotes.

"All proceeded as it must," continued the Po-Matoran. "Until the night the Rahi saw the great red star. That, he decided, must be a wonderful, delicious piece of fruit dangling from some far-off tree. So he climbed the mountain again, and this time he got a running start and jumped with all his might."

Kazi frowned. It was bad enough when Velika got started on one of these stories. It was worse when Kazi got drawn into them and had to find out the end. "So what happened?"

Velika started, as if suddenly remembering that the story had to have an ending. "Oh, what happened? What happened, let's see . . . oh, yes, he went off the cliff and broke every bone in his body."

Kazi immediately began using the old Ko-Matoran trick of counting to himself to prevent an explosion of temper. With Velika, he sometimes reached numbers in the high seven digits.

"Even I am not sure what that one means," admitted Piruk.

"The Rahi fooled himself once, and found only frustration," explained Garan. "But when he fooled himself twice . . . that was far worse."

"He's saying they're not Toa," said Dalu.

Garan shook his head. "He's saying we can't take the chance of being wrong again. If they are Toa, we will apologize later, when they recover. For now, ready your weapons — we attack."

# TWO

Balta sank down to the floor of the cave. How long had he been in here? Hours? Days? He had lost track of time quickly after discovering that the Piraka had trapped him and left him to die.

He had been fleeing Thok and Vezok when he ducked inside the cavern. Finding a good hiding place, he waited, planning to ambush whichever Piraka came in looking for him. Vezok entered, did a quick search, and left before Balta could spring his trap. To the Matoran's surprise, the Piraka had then rolled a huge boulder over the mouth of the cave, sealing him inside.

He knew I was in here. He just didn't know where, and he wasn't going to go exploring, Balta thought. *There isn't any other way out of here. Air's already getting thin. I hope the others escaped, at least. . . .*

Balta closed his eyes and began to drift into unconsciousness. He wondered if Dalu and the others were searching for him. Even if they were, it wouldn't matter. They would never be able to move that boulder. Balta doubted if even Garan's pulse bolts could demolish it in time.

A sharp crack suddenly punctuated his thoughts. At first, he thought someone might be striking the boulder. Then he realized the sound hadn't come from that direction, but rather from the cave wall. An instant later, there was another crack and the wall actually split in two. Balta caught a brief flash of what looked like a massive axe blade slicing through the stone.

Oh, I get it, he said to himself. *I've lost my mind.*

"Well, what are you waiting for, Naming Day?" said a deep, rumbling voice. "Get out of there!"

Balta got up and peered through the crevice. A tunnel extended well beyond it, but it showed no signs of having been dug. Instead, it looked as if the stone had been cleaved. A huge figure, axe in hand, was standing there waiting for him, but it was too dark to make out his features.

"Go and find a place to hide," the figure said. "The Piraka are in complete control of the island. Next time they spot you, Balta, they won't trap you . . . they will kill you."

"Who are you?" asked the Matoran, stepping into the tunnel. "How do you know my name?"

"Let us just say I am a friend," said the massive figure. "A friend who wishes he could do more to help right now, but even my powers are limited. Go. Get to your companions and tell them to stay out of the Piraka's way."

Balta did as he was bid, but shook his head as he ran. "I can do the first, but not the last," he called back. "They have captured our home, and we will take it back!"

"Then at least stop them from making the terrible mistake they soon will make, Balta. Or else, I tell you truly, they will be cursed in the sight of Mata Nui for all time."

The mighty figure watched the Matoran

run off. The villagers would sacrifice everything for each other, even their lives, in an effort to free Voya Nui. Sadly, he reflected on a time when he, too, had had a friend for whom he would have given his life. But that was past now, or soon would be. All he had left was the cause he believed in.

And that I will never surrender, he thought grimly. *Not so long as the Great Spirit Mata Nui lives.*

Far from Voya Nui, Jaller had at last run out of patience.

"Takanuva! Takanuva!" he called into the dark tunnel mouth. Behind him, the other five Matoran watched uneasily.

"Maybe he's hurt," said Hahli. "We should go in after him."

"Not unprotected," said Nuparu. "Give me a few minutes and maybe I can put something together. I brought my tools with me."

"We haven't got a few minutes," said Jaller. "Kongu, Hewkii, come with me. Hahli, Matoro, Nuparu, give us thirty seconds and then you follow. Make sure your lightstones are lit, and stay together."

The three Matoran stepped into the shadows of the tunnel. Instantly, the glow of their lightstones vanished. Curious and concerned, Hahli took a few steps forward and extended her lightstone into the tunnel. As soon as it entered the mouth, its illumination disappeared. Then she withdrew it, only to find it still as bright as before.

"Now, that's weird," she said.

"Here," said Nuparu, extending a length of cable to her. "I salvaged this from the ruins in Metru Nui. Loop the cable around your waist so we three are linked together. Once we're inside, keep talking. If light doesn't work in there, then we can follow the sound of your voice."

Hahli turned and started inside the tunnel. Matoro's words stopped her. "Hahli, before we go in . . . there's something . . . Turaga Nuju said something."

The Ga-Matoran turned. Matoro had been Nuju's translator for centuries and was bound by an oath never to repeat anything he learned as a result of that position. For him to even consider breaking that oath, it had to be something serious.

Matoro took a deep breath and let it out slowly. "Nuju said they sent the Toa to Voya Nui in canisters, like the ones they used to come to Mata Nui. He said there was no other safe way for them to make the journey. He said . . . he said the way to Voya Nui passes through a land of the dead."

Hahli reached out to put a comforting hand on his arm. "Matoro, the Turaga speak in riddles sometimes. You know that. I've rowed through winding streams that were straighter than their words, most times. There is no 'land of the dead,' any more than there is some hidden paradise called Artakha. They are just legends, my friend. Now, let's go."

Matoro nodded and fell into step behind Nuparu. But he couldn't help thinking how frequently the legends told by Turaga turned out to be all too painfully true.

As soon as he crossed the threshold into

the tunnel, Matoro's lightstone went out. The same had obviously happened to the others, as he was surrounded by complete darkness. Despite Nuparu's advice, Hahli was staying silent, which Matoro found unnerving.

"Speak up!" he shouted. "Where are you?" At least, those are the words his mouth formed, but no sound emerged. He reached down and felt the cable around his waist — yes, it was still there, and still taut. The others had to be up ahead of him.

He stumbled forward in the darkness, once almost tripping on a rock. He stuck his arm out and could feel the stone wall to the side, but could not find Nuparu in front of him. If it had not been for the cable, he would have felt hopelessly lost, alone, desperate, and maybe even panicked. As it was, at least he didn't feel alone.

He stumbled again, this time over something that felt alive. He reached down and felt someone grab his hand. Matoro smiled. It felt good to make physical contact with one of his friends, even if they couldn't see each other or speak.

He helped the prone figure to his feet and held tight to his hand, trying to lead him out of the darkness.

Matoro felt a tug on the cable, then another. He picked up the pace, still guiding his unseen friend. Around a corner, he spotted light — wonderful light, glorious light! There were Hahli, Nuparu, Takanuva, Jaller . . . and Hewkii . . . and Kongu . . . and . . .

And if they are all there . . . whose hand am I holding?

Matoro turned quickly even as he felt the hand in his slip away. There was no one to be seen. He turned back to his friends, looking down at his hand and trying not to show how shaken he felt.

"What is it? You look upset," said Hahli.

"Just . . . missing someone," he replied, not looking up at her. "Or some . . . thing."

"What do you mean, you left the Toa on the slope?" Zaktan hissed. The emerald-armored leader of the Piraka looked from one of his team to the other, his expression daring them to speak.

"What were we supposed to do?" Vezok finally growled. "Stand there and burn with them? The lava was heading right for them. By now they're charred armor, and not much else."

Zaktan's eyes glowed red. Twin lasers shot from them and struck Vezok. The impact of the blow knocked the Piraka across the room and seared a hole in his shoulder armor.

"You were supposed to follow your orders," said Zaktan in a deathly quiet tone. "Getting rid of those Toa Nuva was more important than your miserable lives. I would gladly have sacrificed the five of you to be rid of the six of them."

"We like you, too," muttered Avak.

"These are Toa," Zaktan continued. "It was Toa who defeated the Dark Hunters when we attempted to conquer Metru Nui. It was Toa who engineered the war between us and the Brotherhood of Makuta that still rages today. Leaving a Toa, any Toa, alive is like keeping a doom viper for companionship."

"Hey, we've all fought Toa before," growled Reidak. "Some of us even look forward to it. But like Vezok said, they're dead. Ashes. I'm sure of it."

Zaktan allowed the microscopic protodites that made up his body to drift apart until he resembled a dark cloud hovering over the Piraka. When he spoke, his voice seemed to come from everywhere at once. "I remember the last time you were 'sure,' Reidak. Do you?"

The cloud drifted toward the vat of anti-dermis, the strange substance that had transformed Voya Nui's Matoran into hollow-eyed slaves. "Once, we were seven, or have you forgotten?" Zaktan continued. "Our seventh member discovered the existence of the Mask of Life along with us, and the clues to where it was hidden. You were sure, Reidak, that he would not betray us. You were wrong.

"He came to this island on his own, in secret, determined to brave the fires of the volcano and steal the mask." The protodites drifted together once more, forming a body for Zaktan. He grinned evilly. "And he never returned."

"Perhaps he found the mask," said Hakann. "Did you ever think of that?"

Zaktan stared off into space for a moment. When next he spoke, the multitude of voices that usually came from his lips had been joined by one other, a guttural growl none of the Piraka had ever heard before. "No," he said. "If the Mask of Life had been found . . . I would know."

None of the Piraka were sure whether they believed Zaktan. At the same time, none were foolish enough to openly disagree with him. After a few moments, he turned his attention back to them.

"How many Matoran died in the eruption?"

"Too many," said Thok. "Work has stopped completely on some parts of the mountain. The lava is only being drained out of the volcano at half the rate of before."

"Hakann, make them work harder," ordered Zaktan. "Make an example of some of them if you believe it will pierce their dull brains. Avak, you remain here with me. The rest of you — find the Toa Nuva. Kill them. If there is a Toa still alive at sundown . . . you won't be."

Hakann, Thok, Vezok, and Reidak filed out of the chamber. Thok glanced over his shoulder and saw Zaktan already deep in conversation with Avak. "What do you think they're talking about?"

"Doom. Destruction. The end of all existence," said Hakann, sounding bored. "You know Zaktan, always great company."

"Remind me," said Vezok, nursing his wounded shoulder. "Was he always the hindquarters of a Muaka, or is this something new?"

Reidak shook his head. "He's worse now. Ever since we went to Metru Nui and found Makuta's shattered armor, he's been a little . . . on edge. He stopped caring about loot, or even grabbing a city for ourselves. All he wanted was the Mask of Life."

Hakann chuckled. "Mask of Life for him," he said. "But death, perhaps, for all of us?"

THREE

"Anyone who wants to turn back, now is the time," said Jaller. Stretching before them was a long, narrow strip of land, flanked on either side by a violent sea. In the distance, they could see a natural stone archway, and beyond that, a winding, torturous path between two peaks.

"Right, I want to quick-go back through that tunnel again," Kongu said, sarcastically. "I haven't had that much fun since I rode a Gukko that had hiccups."

"We shouldn't waste time," said Hahli. "If we are going, then let's go."

The group began walking again. Takanuva hung back to walk beside the Ga-Matoran. "You seem uncertain about all this, Hahli."

"I am," she replied. "As the Chronicler, it's my job to record the adventures of Toa . . . just as it was your job before me. Now I'm afraid the last chronicle I write will be obituaries for us all."

Takanuva nodded. "Maybe. I don't agree with how Jaller did this, but I do see why he acted. If we did nothing, you would be writing a last tribute to the entire universe, Hahli, not just six Matoran and one novice Toa."

"You're not a novice," Hahli said, with a little smile. "You beat Makuta, after all."

"I got lucky," said the Toa of Light. "His pride made him want to challenge me one-on-one, his shadow versus my light. If he had used the other powers he commands, well, things might have turned out differently. You know, I glimpsed his mind when we were briefly merged into one being. . . . It's a labyrinth, all twists and turns and places that have seen no light in centuries."

"You still defeated him," said Hahli. "Your light was stronger than his darkness."

Takanuva shrugged. "Or he let me win. Maybe he thought it was inevitable that we would make our way back to Metru Nui eventually, so he decided to pick the time. Maybe the whole thing was just part of some bigger plot."

Hahli looked up at the Toa, puzzled. "Bigger?"

"I'm just guessing, but what if . . . what if he hatched a plan so deadly that it wouldn't matter if the Matoran returned to Metru Nui or not? What if, in the end, he decided that carrying out that plan mattered more than beating me?"

"If you're right, I don't think much of his planning skills," said Hahli. "After all, he got himself killed, remember?"

"It certainly seemed that way," Takanuva replied. "Didn't it?"

Their conversation was cut short by a shout from Hewkii. The Po-Matoran was up ahead, trying to pry something out of the ground. Exerting all his strength, he finally tore it loose, only to go tumbling over backward from the effort. He sprang up, holding his prize in his hands: a dirt-encrusted, slightly battered Kanohi mask. Smiling, he took off his own mask and slipped the new one on, only to remove it almost instantly.

"It's a Great Mask!" he said. "I could feel the power in it."

Takanuva took it from him and examined it. "I don't recognize the design. Turaga Vakama might, though. I wonder what it does."

Before any could protest, he removed his Mask of Light and put on Hewkii's find. At first, nothing happened. Then Takanuva suddenly said, "I am not taking too many chances, Hahli."

"What?" said the Ga-Matoran. "What are you talking about?"

"You said I was taking a risk by putting this mask on. I heard you."

"I never said anything!" Hahli protested.

"She's telling the truth," said Hewkii. "Maybe it has something to do with the mask. . . . Maybe it's defective?"

"Or maybe it works just fine," said Jaller. "Hahli, be honest — what were you thinking when he put the mask on?"

The Ga-Matoran shrugged, obviously uncomfortable. "I was thinking . . . well . . . that we only have one Toa with us and he shouldn't be braving any unnecessary dangers."

"You heard her thoughts," Jaller said to Takanuva. "It's a Mask of Telepathy. It must have belonged to some other Toa who passed this way, who knows how long ago."

"Passed this way, or never went any farther than this?" asked the Toa of Light, quickly replacing the mask with his own. "What are the odds the rest of that Toa is underneath our feet?"

Jaller didn't answer. There wasn't any need.

The Matoran camped about three-quarters of the way to the archway. Jaller stood watch while Hahli, Hewkii, Nuparu, and Kongu slept. Takanuva had wandered off by himself. Periodically, Jaller would pause to take a closer look at the Kanohi mask they had found and wonder what sort of Toa had worn it.

Matoro had tried to sleep, but could not. He finally gave up trying and went to join Jaller. "Anything?"

Jaller shook his head. "Just rocks and water. I don't even see any Rahi. How about you?"

"No, I don't see anything, either."

"I was asking about what you *didn't* see," said Jaller. "Back in the tunnel . . . something obviously rattled you in there."

"We're someplace we're not supposed to be," Matoro replied, looking away. "That's all."

"You could have said the same about Mata Nui," said Jaller. "We were never meant to live there. We should have been on Metru Nui all those years. Makuta's crimes threw the universe off balance. We're making this journey to try and right it."

"What if that's not possible?" asked the Ko-Matoran. "What if things have just been wrong for too long? I mean, look at this place! Nothing lives here; I doubt anything ever could. This place is dead, Jaller, and if we stay here, then we might be —"

"Jaller!"

The two Matoran turned to see Takanuva

running toward them. "A Matoran!" he shouted. "I just saw a Matoran inside the archway!"

The others had awakened due to the commotion. Now they gathered around as the Toa of Light shared his experience. "I was walking along the coastline, wondering about the Toa who had worn that mask. Then I glanced up and there he was — a Matoran I had never seen before. He looked at me from the other side of the archway, with fear in his eyes. I used a fraction of my power, just enough to create a soft glow, but before I could say anything, he ran."

Jaller frowned. What was a Matoran doing way out here? The same thing they were? Or was there more going on than any of them were aware of?

"Come on. Let's find him," he said finally. "No one should be alone in this desolation."

"How do we know he's alone?" asked Kongu as they started for the archway.

"How do we know he's even a Matoran?" Matoro added.

"Well, what else could he be?"

Remembering the hand holding his in the tunnel, Matoro answered, "Oh, you don't want to know."

Takanuva led the way back to the archway, Jaller and Hewkii close behind. There was no sign of any Matoran or anything else up ahead. Matoro glanced around as he ran, just to make sure something wasn't using this sighting as bait for an ambush.

"This way!" yelled the Toa of Light as he approached the stone arch. An instant later, he went flying backward, crashing into the Matoran behind him. Shaken, he got to his feet and ran toward the archway again. As soon as he reached the threshold, he slammed into an invisible barrier and was knocked to the ground.

Now he was angry. Rising, he hurled two narrow beams of light at the unseen obstacle. They ricocheted wildly, almost burning a hole through Kongu.

"Watch it!" snapped the Le-Matoran. "We're on the same side, remember?"

Nuparu took a few steps toward the archway, then stopped. Cautiously, he reached out and felt . . . nothing at all. Puzzled, he took another step, and passed right through as if no barrier were there.

Emboldened by the sight, Takanuva went to follow him. But for him, nothing had changed, because he still could not get through. "I don't understand this," he said, frustrated. "What lets a Matoran through, but bars a Toa?"

The other five Matoran hesitantly crossed under the archway, leaving Takanuva the only one still on the other side. Jaller tried to go back and join him, but now found the barrier stopped him from returning the way he had come.

"Explain this," said the Ta-Matoran to Nuparu.

The Onu-Matoran inventor shook his head. "There's nothing mechanical inside the stone, at least as far as I can tell. There's no sign of a power source. The barrier is there, but I can't explain why."

"Maybe I can." The words came from Hahli,

who was holding a small stone tablet in her hand. "I found this on the ground, not far from here. It's ancient, almost unbelievably so. Turaga Nuju showed me some of the marker stones kept in the Ko-Metru Knowledge Towers, and based on the carvings and symbols on this . . . it was made before Metru Nui even existed."

"Can you read it?" asked Kongu.

"A few months ago, I would have said no," replied Hahli. "But Nokama has been teaching me. She says I used to know how to do this, I just forgot. Anyway, let me try."

Hahli studied the tablet for a few minutes. She started to say something, then stopped and gave it some more thought. "It's a warning," she reported. "It reads something like . . . 'This is a realm of shadow . . . of famine and plague and blight. . . . This is a world of darkness . . . and there is no place for light.'"

Nuparu nodded. "Of course. It makes sense now."

"To you, maybe," said Hewkii. "All I see is,

whoever is in charge of attracting tourists here is doing a lousy job."

"I thought that tunnel we went through was just a natural phenomenon, something that doused lightstones. Now I'm wondering if maybe all illumination wasn't actually being devoured. And if that wasn't enough to send a bearer of light running home, we come here, where light is actively repelled."

"Okay, but what about us? Why can't we get back through?" asked Matoro. "We don't have the power of light; only Takanuva does."

"I think the answer to that one is frighteningly simple," said Nuparu. "Someone, or something, doesn't want us to leave."

"This is insane," said the Toa of Light. "You can't keep going, Jaller. It's a trap. Stay where you are, and I'll find some way through that barrier."

"I don't think you will, old friend," said Jaller. "Not if it was built to keep you out. Go back to Metru Nui and tell the Turaga what has happened. Tell them . . . tell them not to send any help. We'll keep moving and hopefully find the Toa Nuva somewhere up ahead."

Takanuva reached out for his lifelong friend, but the barrier got in the way. "I can't even shake your hand good-bye," he said sadly. "This could be the last time I ever see you, and I can't shake your hand."

"We'll see each other again," said Jaller. "After all, who is going to keep you out of trouble if not me?"

"And Toa get into much bigger trouble than Matoran . . . most of the time, anyway," the Toa of Light said, trying to smile. "Hey, Jaller, you . . . I mean, you already died once for me. Don't die again, okay? It would make for a lousy chronicle, the same thing happening a second time and all."

Jaller smiled and turned away, trying to hide his own emotions. After a moment, he said to the other Matoran, "Come on, we have to keep going. If something is after us, there's no point in being a sitting target."

The small group said their good-byes to

Takanuva. Hahli couldn't even get the words out, just pressed her hand against the barrier to meet Takanuva's. Then the party began walking away.

"Jaller!" Takanuva shouted. The Ta-Matoran turned around. "Destiny should have chosen you to be the Toa of Light. You would make a great Toa."

"Thanks, but no, thanks," Jaller replied. "It's tough enough just being a Matoran."

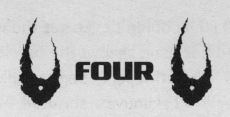

FOUR

This, Lewa Nuva decided, had been the worst day of his life.

Bad enough to run into six Makuta wannabes who smiled while they were pounding you into oblivion, and having one of his air katana snapped in the process. Even more disturbing was being defeated and losing his Kanohi mask, along with those of the other Toa Nuva. But now the six most powerful heroes in the universe — at least, in his opinion — were under attack by five very angry Matoran.

And worse — we're losing! he thought.

"Nice bunch of villagers they have here," he muttered, ducking under a pulse bolt. "I don't think they much crave-need protection. I think we do."

Tahu Nuva threw up a wall of flame, temporarily cutting the Toa off from their attackers.

"What do you want us to do?" he snapped. "Unleash our elemental powers and maybe kill them? Our best bet is to stall for time until we can find a way to prove to them who we are."

"When did you become so cautious?" asked Lewa.

"Maybe I've grown up," answered Tahu. "And before you question the wisdom of that, I'd remind you that I'm not the one missing a Toa tool because he charged into battle not knowing what he was up against."

"Enough!" yelled Gali. "You may have grown smarter, Tahu, but evidently your mouth hasn't shared in the learning. And as for you, Lewa — aaaaahh!"

Gali Nuva suddenly dropped to the ground, hands clamped over her eyes. An instant before, Dalu had used her bizarre abilities to enhance Gali's sight far beyond its upper limits. For a brief moment, she could see everything — every atom, every molecule, from Voya Nui across the entire plane of existence. Then her sight pierced into other dimensions as well, places where concepts of time and space as she knew them had no meaning. She had immediately closed her eyes tight, but even through the protective lids, she could still see!

"So much . . . so beautiful . . . and so terrible . . . ," she cried. "Beyond anything even the Great Beings could imagine . . ."

"What's wrong with her?" said Pohatu, kneeling beside the Toa Nuva of Water.

"I don't know," said Kopaka quietly. "But I can only guess those Matoran are somehow responsible."

The Toa of Ice started forward, heedless of the wall of fire. Tahu reached out to stop him, but Kopaka shrugged him off. "I have had enough," said the master of the winter storm. "And more than enough."

To Tahu's amazement, Kopaka proceeded to walk through the fire. If he felt pain, he showed no sign of it. The Toa of Fire immediately doused the barrier and watched as his brother Toa marched toward their attackers.

Pulse bolts and hurled boulders struck him dead-on, but never once did he waver.

"Back him up," Tahu told the others.

"But you said —" Lewa began.

Tahu cut him off with a heated glare. "I said *back him up.*"

He glanced up to see that Kopaka really needed no help. The usually cool and collected Toa had given in to an icy rage that showed no signs of abating. He had already flash-frozen three of the villagers, with only the Ga-Matoran and Onu-Matoran still fighting.

"Do it while they are still alive," Tahu said. Pohatu, Onua, and Lewa dutifully charged forward, as much to restrain their fellow Toa as to fight their attackers.

Tahu cradled Gali in his arms. Once, when he had been poisoned by a Rahkshi and driven to violence against his friends, it had been Gali who fought to bring him back. It had been her healing powers that had helped to save him. He had no such abilities — fire destroyed, it did not create or heal — but he would not leave her side, not until this crisis had passed.

Her eyelids flickered and then opened. But the light in her eyes was different now, and frighteningly so. Tahu imagined it was how his must have looked when he was sickened and out of control. One glance was enough to see that madness had claimed Gali Nuva.

"I can still see!" she shouted. Before he could react, she had summoned a fist of water from thin air and slammed him with it. Then she sprang up and ran headlong away from him, back in the direction of the volcano. He jumped up and started after her, realizing with dread that she was running straight for the Piraka.

Behind him, the Matoran and the three Toa Nuva were at a standoff. Left to his own devices, Kopaka would have long since ended the battle. But Onua and Lewa had intervened and kept him from using killing force on those the Toa had vowed to protect. Now heroes and villagers stared at each other, waiting for someone to make a move. Only a few yards separated them physically, but the gulf between them was vast just the same.

"Who are you?" said Garan. "And don't try to tell me you are some new kind of Toa. I have heard that one before and it cost me almost all of my friends."

"Whether you believe it or not does not alter the facts," replied Onua. "We are Toa Nuva, from the island of Mata Nui."

Garan snorted in derision. "Toa what? Island of what? Not only are you lying, they are not even good lies. There is no such thing as a Toa Nuva . . . and no island of Mata Nui exists, or we would know of it. You are allies of the Piraka, aren't you, come to help them subjugate our brothers and sisters?"

"The Piraka are no heart-friends of ours," said Lewa. "We have been fighting them."

"A falling-out among thieves," spat Dalu. "I say we take them, Garan, starting with frosty over there."

The four Toa Nuva readied for battle. Garan and Dalu did the same, even knowing they had little chance of victory. Both sides teetered on the precipice of tragedy, neither willing to lower their weapons and back away.

"Wait! Stop!" The Matoran and Toa turned to see Balta running at top speed down a rocky slope. Dalu broke into a grin, confident that with her Ta-Matoran friend present, they might win after all.

"Another one," grumbled Lewa. "We are going to spend all day fighting Matoran, while the Piraka wander free."

"No one is going to fight anyone," Balta said to him. He turned to his friends and said, "You're making a mistake. These aren't our enemies. I am not sure who they are, but I know that a battle now would be a terrible error."

Garan looked at Balta closely. He showed none of the signs of being controlled by the Piraka. The Onu-Matoran wanted to believe that these strange, maskless beings were potential allies, but he needed more than just Balta's word. The realization saddened him. There was a time when any statement of fact by any Matoran would have gone unquestioned, but the Piraka had brought many changes to Voya Nui.

Sensing the moment of crisis was at hand, Onua Nuva threw his quake-breakers onto the ground. Then he removed his Nuva armor and tossed that aside as well. "There. No mask. No weapons. No extra armor. I've seen what your pulse bolts can do, Matoran, so use one now if you want war so badly. Kill me and my friends, and see if it gets you anywhere nearer to freeing your island from evil."

Garan looked up at the stranger. If he was a Toa, then his black armor marked him as a Toa of Earth, the protector of Onu-Matoran everywhere. He had the power to down both Matoran with one swing of his mighty arm, yet he was leaving himself open to attack. The Matoran considered, nodded, and then threw his own weapons on the ground as well.

"What are you doing?" Dalu protested.

"What someone had to do," Balta told her.

"We already have a battle on our hands, one that has been thrust upon us. We don't need to go looking for another."

"I think we have much to talk about," said Onua Nuva. "Starting with anything you know about these Piraka, anything that might be a key to defeating them."

The notion of defeated Piraka was very much on Hakann's mind as well. Despite Zaktan's orders, the crimson-armored Piraka had no intention of scrambling over this pile of rock to search for escaped Toa Nuva. He would sooner have frolicked in the surf with hungry Takea sharks.

Instead, he doubled back and made his way to the stronghold. As he expected, Zaktan was already there, once more muttering in low tones to the vat of virus that dominated the central chamber. At times, Zaktan acted like that container of viscous goo was his best friend in the world.

Well, it's certainly his only friend, Hakann thought. *But what do they "talk" about, I wonder?*

He crept closer, staying to the shadows. Hakann's eyes widened at the sight he beheld. Zaktan was not alone in the chamber, but was deep in conversation with a powerful armored figure who looked like he could snap a Toa in two with no effort at all. He was tall, clad in blue and gold armor, and wielded a twin-bladed sword. There was something about the stranger's mask that made even the hardened Piraka shudder.

As Hakann watched, Zaktan fired one of the zamor spheres into the mysterious giant. Strangely, the sphere did not seem to have its usual effect of sapping the will. In fact, the giant actually appeared to be stronger and fiercer after absorbing the virus into his system.

Zaktan spoke again, in words too soft to hear. The giant nodded and departed. Hakann wasted no time in making his own way out of the stronghold and picking up the newcomer's trail. If the leader of the Piraka had found a secret weapon in this powerhouse figure, Hakann wanted to know about it.

*   *   *

Zaktan watched his newest pawn leave. Then he remained very still, as if lost in thought, until Hakann had left, too. Of course he had known that the treacherous Piraka was present and spying. He would not have lasted long as leader of this murderous little band if he did not always know what was going on around him.

Now Hakann would follow the colossus named Brutaka in an effort to discover his identity and connection to Zaktan. And with any luck at all, his curiosity would be satisfied . . . maybe even before his existence was terminated.

Gali Nuva had lost track of how long she had been running. She didn't know where she was or why she was here. Even if someone had explained it all to her, it would have done no good, for her mind was aflame with madness. No rational thought need apply.

There was no plan behind her flight. If allowed to, she would run until she reached the shore and then swim until her arms and legs grew so tired she sank to the bottom.

It was only the sight of a powerful figure standing in her path that brought her to a halt. She didn't recognize him, but he looked like an enemy. Certainly the huge axe he carried did not spark trust. She gave a yell of rage and launched a water blast so powerful it would tear the armor off a foe.

The figure waited a moment or two, then swatted the blast away with his axe as if it were no more than an annoyance. Before Gali could attack again, he was in front of her, reaching out to touch her maskless face.

"Your friends have need of you," he said. "And by the power of Mata Nui, you will return to them, whole and sane."

Pure power flowed from him into the Toa Nuva of Water. The madness and pain fell away in an instant, leaving her sharp mind intact. Only the memories of what had driven her to madness were blocked off from her.

"Who are you?" she asked.

The figure backed away. "Go back to your comrades. They will be worried for you. If it is the will of Mata Nui, we will meet again."

Gali Nuva was tempted to ask more questions, or even follow her newfound friend. But something in his manner said that neither would be welcome. Instead, she turned back and headed for the scene of the Toa Nuva–Matoran struggle. Her madness may have been gone, but there was a great deal more insanity on this island to be confronted and overcome.

 **FIVE**

Kongu paused, stretched his aching muscles, and gazed up at the summit in the distance. He, Jaller, and the others had been following a winding trail up a mountainside for what felt like days. More than once, they had believed they were near the top, only to reach a plateau and find the rock extended several hundred feet higher up.

"I don't have any hope-faith that there is a peak to this mountain," he muttered. "I think it just goes up and up until we are mask-to-mask with Mata Nui himself."

"Then maybe we can talk to him about sleeping on the job," Nuparu answered. "If I had the right materials, you know, I could make us some climbing gear. We'd be at the top in no time."

Hewkii shook his head. "You miners and tree swingers are out of shape. In Po-Koro, we used to climb pebbles like this every day, just for the view."

Kongu glanced at his companion in disbelief. Hewkii managed to hold a serious expression for only a few seconds before breaking into a grin.

"Only thing worse than a Po-Matoran carver is a Po-Matoran carver with a sense of humor," said Nuparu, laughing.

A scuttling sound above and to the right brought the chatter and the laughter to an abrupt halt. Kongu bounded up the slope and looked around. Then he turned back to the others and shrugged. "I don't see anything," he whispered.

Matoro caught up to the others. He had obviously heard the sound as well. "Maybe we should head back down? Find another way to where we're going?"

"There is no other way," said Hewkii. "Kongu and I already looked. It's up the mountain or nothing."

Jaller and Hahli approached, talking in hushed tones. The Ta-Matoran was scanning the rocks with his keen eyes, searching for movement. He found none. "We'll keep going, but carefully," he decided. "What we all heard might just be some Rahi, or it might mean there is someone else here. Maybe even the same someone responsible for the Toa Nuva's disappearance."

"So we walk into a trap?" asked Hahli, resuming the climb.

"No," replied Jaller. "We just make sure we spring it ourselves."

The next hour was spent hiking up the mountain with periodic stops for rest. The scuttling sounds had become more frequent as they climbed higher, until they became almost constant. They obviously came from something large, but it remained unseen, a fact that bothered Nuparu.

"It doesn't make sense," the Onu-Matoran said. "How can a creature so big stay out of sight?"

"Ever try to catch a dermis turtle when it doesn't want to be caught?" said Hahli. "They're slow, but they know their home territory — every rock, every patch of seaweed. They can hide for days while you swim over, around, and past them."

"So we're being stalked by a really big turtle?" asked Kongu.

The harsh, clattering sound of something scrambling across the rocks came again, this time almost on top of them. At about the same time, Jaller pointed to the rocks just above them. A lone Matoran was peering down at them, close enough for the party to get a good look. His mask, in the shape of a Kanohi Rau, was weathered and dented in numerous places. His armor was scratched and discolored. Most striking of all, his left arm was badly damaged and hung limply at his side.

"Who are you?" Hahli shouted to the Matoran. "Come down and maybe we can help you."

The figure never moved, just stared at her with frightened eyes.

"If he's not coming down, we'll have to go up," said Jaller. "Slowly, all, let's try not to scare him off."

Moving casually, the six Matoran made their way up the slope. Jaller held out his arms, palms up, to show he carried no weapons. Hahli forced herself to smile. None of it seemed to make any difference to their new companion.

"Do you think there is something wrong with him?" whispered Kongu.

"He lives here," Hewkii replied. "So I'd say that's a good guess."

When they were within about five paces of the Matoran, the scuttling noises returned, this time from both sides. Jaller threw up his hand to halt the group just as the source of the sounds made themselves visible. Two monstrous crabs emerged from the rocks to flank the silent Matoran, followed by two more, and then two more. Although no one in Jaller's party had ever seen such a thing before, they all knew what they were from tales told by the Toa.

"Manas," Hahli said, shocked.

"This is impossible," said Matoro. "The Toa said there were only two of them, and they were driven off. Toa Onua encountered one later on and survived to tell the story. How can there be six?"

Two more Manas appeared now, moving

to stand by the others. The Matoran they crowded near appeared to take no notice of them.

"Eight," said Hewkii. "And maybe Toa can't count?"

"We need a plan," said Matoro.

"Would screaming and running count?" asked Kongu. "'Cause that seems like a really good plan right now."

The silent Matoran took a step forward, gestured for the others to follow, then turned and began to walk up the slope. After a moment, the Manas turned and started after him. Jaller's group stood for a moment, puzzled, before Hahli began to follow as well.

"What are you doing?" asked Nuparu. "You're going in the direction of the Manas!"

"I'm the Chronicler," she answered, not looking back. "Finding answers is part of my job."

The six Matoran did not have to travel far. Their strange guide and the Manas led them into a bowl-shaped canyon. All around, they saw Matoran in various stages of disrepair, many of them vastly different in size and mask style from those Jaller was familiar with. They regarded the newcomers with hollow, haunted eyes. As the small party passed by, these wounded Matoran fell into step behind them, moving silently like an army of ghosts.

"What is this place?" asked Nuparu. "It looks like one of Makuta's daydreams."

"All of these Matoran look frightened," said Jaller. "No, beyond frightened . . . resigned . . . like they lost hope long, long ago."

"Can't say I blame them," remarked Hahli. "Look up ahead."

The metal structure she pointed to might have once been a landmark to rival the Metru Nui Coliseum. Now it was a charred, twisted ruin whose towers reached up like claws eager to rend the sky. Dull fires burned within, but there was nothing welcoming about their glow.

An explosion suddenly rocked the canyon. Jaller and the others turned to see a small volcano erupting to the east. Amazingly, it spewed chunks of ice into the air that flew high and then landed with a crash. Matoro approached one of the frozen missiles and reached out to touch it, only to pull his hand back with a cry.

"It's hot!"

Jaller touched a fingertip to the ice and drew it back quickly. "He's right. This ice is searing. But at such a temperature, it should melt . . . shouldn't it?"

Hahli gave a shout. They turned to see her standing knee-deep in a pool of water, staring wide-eyed at a "waterfall" consisting completely of dust. It billowed over the rocks, an arid brown cloud, but where it came from, she could not tell.

"Why do I think that if we find a fire here, it will freeze us?" said Nuparu. "Or that the only thing that might fall from the clouds above is a hail of stones?"

"Let's see if we can set a record for fastest to get out of this place," said Matoro.

A violent flash of lightning ripped through the sky overhead, but no thunder accompanied it. A few moments later, a gentle breeze rippled the water of the pond, producing an earsplitting thunderclap.

"Okay, that does it," said Jaller. "There has to be a way through or around this canyon and we're finding it."

The group turned to leave the way they had come, only to find a half dozen Manas blocking their way. More of the monstrous crabs were now lining the rim of the canyon as well, silently regarding the newcomers. The only way open to the Matoran was forward.

It was not an easy trek. At one point, they passed through what seemed like a statuary garden, with stone sculptures of Matoran everywhere. When they started to move on, they discovered that the rock beneath their feet screamed with each step. The sounds so unnerved the party that they stopped dead.

"Maybe we should just wait here until we wake up," said Hahli. "Because this has to be a bad dream."

"It is indeed a dream, little Matoran . . . and the last one you will ever know."

The words came from a huge armored figure who blocked their path up ahead. Like the fortress from which he had emerged, he was battered and twisted and his mask looked as if it had been patched together from three or four different ones. His ebon and gold armor was studded with razor-sharp blades, and his gauntlets crackled with energy. In one hand he held a burning length of chain. His eyes were a deep, hollow black, and when he spoke, his voice was surprisingly quiet, as if he had not used it for a very long time.

"Who are you?" asked Hewkii. "What kind of crazy place is this?"

The powerful figure smiled. "This is my home . . . and now yours as well. It has been many, many centuries since any Matoran came here. You are most welcome. As for who I am, you may call me Karzahni."

The name seemed familiar to the Matoran, but they could not place it at first. Then Hahli whispered, "I knew I had heard that name before. It was in one of Turaga Vakama's tales. He said there was an ancient legend that Matoran who were poor workers were sent to a place of darkness ruled by a being called Karzahni . . . and none of them ever returned."

Jaller nodded. "And later, Makuta named one of his plant creatures 'Karzahni' as his private joke. But the original tale was just a legend, I thought."

"You should know by now," replied Kongu. "Matoran legends are usually true and always lethal."

"Sad, but true," added Hahli. "As Chronicler, I have written down my share, and it tends to be grim work."

Karzahni spoke again. "Long ago . . . perhaps 100,000 years, perhaps more, I lose track . . . Matoran came here by the score. Some were damaged, others simply possessed a lack of dedication to their work. A small number found a new life here . . . and the rest found only what they had expected, which was nothing at all."

"These Matoran don't look like they are enjoying their 'new life' very much," Hahli remarked.

Karzahni smiled. "I suppose they find it preferable to the alternative . . . as you will, too, no doubt, provided I give you the choice."

"This is monstrous!" snapped Jaller. "I can't believe that the Great Spirit Mata Nui would allow such a place to exist. Even Makuta would not —"

He stopped speaking when he realized Karzahni looked completely confused. "Mata Nui?" said the armored figure. "Makuta? Who are they? And what possible influence would they have here?"

A dozen of Karzahni's Matoran closed in then, stripping the party of their tools, supplies, and even the Kanohi Suletu they had found. Then Karzahni stretched out his arms toward Jaller and the rest, prepared to receive the last and most important things they possessed.

"Your masks," he said. "Take them off."

Jaller shook his head. He had only recently learned that the mask he wore had once belonged to Turaga Lhikan, a great hero of Metru Nui. Lhikan had died to save the Matoran from Makuta.

There was no way Jaller would simply surrender his mask to anyone.

"You can remove them, or I can have them removed," Karzahni continued, his tone growing more menacing. "Decide."

"Try it," said Jaller.

Energy flashed from Karzahni's gauntlet. Jaller braced himself for a physical impact, but there was none. Instead, the world around him melted and shifted until he was back in a place he knew well, reliving a moment he could never forget.

It was Kini Nui, the most sacred site on all of the island of Mata Nui. He and his best friend, Takua, were battling monstrous Rahkshi alongside the Toa Nuva. The Rahkshi Turahk was advancing on Takua, and Jaller knew he had to save his comrade. He knew what was about to happen, for he had already experienced this months ago. He would sacrifice himself to save Takua, who would then don the Mask of Light and become a powerful Toa. The fact that he was eventually brought back to life did not lessen the importance of what Jaller had done that day.

Only now something was different. Jaller was telling himself to run, leap, block the Rahkshi from reaching Takua, but his body was not responding. As if it were happening in slow motion, he saw the Rahkshi blast Takua with concentrated fear energy. His friend screamed, staggered, and then fell dead from sheer fright.

Time shot forward. With Takua dead, the Toa of Light never came to be. The Rahkshi stole the Mask of Light so that there would never be any chance of such a Toa rising against him. Makuta created more and more Rahkshi to send against the island of Mata Nui, until eventually the Toa Nuva were overwhelmed and destroyed. Emboldened by his victory, Makuta himself led the next attack, capturing and imprisoning the Turaga and enslaving the Matoran. Any violation of Makuta's law, or any hesitation in carrying out his orders, was punishable by death. It took only the loss of a few villagers for the rest to decide it made more sense to just obey.

The only glimmer of hope in the next thousand years came when Turaga Onewa led a breakout and it seemed like the village elders might escape. Instead, they ran into a patrol of Rahkshi. Jaller wished he could close his mind's eye and not have to see what happened next. As it was, he was forced to watch every gruesome moment of the battle and its inevitable conclusion.

The final image was the worst of all. He and Hahli, once among the bravest of Matoran, were reduced to being personal servants to Makuta. The expressions on their faces looked far too much like those of Karzahni's Matoran for comfort.

That realization snapped Jaller out of the illusion. He was back in this strange land, surrounded by his friends and confronting his tormentor. But the vision he had seen had done its work. He couldn't easily shake the feelings of despair and hopelessness that it had sparked. He knew he had saved Takua in real life, but now he also knew what it would have been like if he had failed. What if he failed again? What if this time Hahli or Matoro died because he wasn't fast enough? It might be better just not to try anything.

Eyes locked on the ground, as silent as the Matoran of Karzahni's realm, Jaller reached up and took off his mask.

SIX

Hakann had a new theory. This new ally of Zaktan's had a special, secret power: the ability to walk around and around for hours and thoroughly bore any enemies to death.

The Piraka had been following the mysterious figure for hours now, and all he had done had been to wander up and down slopes in a generally westerly direction. There was no sense of urgency or mission about his movements. He seemed like an idle Rahi out for a stroll.

At least, he did until he utterly vanished. One moment he was clearly visible in a flash of lightning, and then the next flash revealed him to be gone. There didn't seem to be any obvious hiding places, yet he was nowhere to be seen. Hakann slowed his pace, every sense on alert. If this was a trap of some kind, he had no intention of being caught in it.

He was right in the middle of congratulating himself on how cautious he was being when he felt the blade at his throat. He had no more idea how his quarry had gotten behind him than he did how someone so big could move so fast and disappear so well.

"Why have you been following me?" The voice of Hakann's captor was harsh and ragged.

"Following you?" repeated Hakann. "Not at all. I was merely out enjoying the scenery."

"What scenery?" the larger being said, tightening his grip. "It's rock all around, until you reach that puny strip of grass and trees by the coast. So I will ask a second time — why are you following me? And if you lie to me again, I will take you apart, very precisely and very slowly . . . just slowly enough so you will be awake for all of it. Do you understand?"

Hakann would have nodded, but it would have meant bringing his throat down on the blade. Instead, he said, "Of course. We have no reason to be enemies, you and I. Our mutual foe is back there in the stronghold."

The stranger released his hold and shoved Hakann forward. The Piraka staggered a few steps and turned, rubbing his throat. "Breathing. I was beginning to miss it," he muttered.

"I thought you were one of Zaktan's servants," said the stranger. "Now you say you oppose him."

"Servant?" Hakann sputtered, almost choking on the word. "Zaktan has a vivid imagination, I see. No, I serve only myself, and so should you. I don't know what he is offering you to ally with him, but I am sure I can make a better deal . . . I'll even give you the honor of killing him."

The stranger laughed bitterly. "My name is Brutaka — I know that has no meaning for you. But, at one time, it meant a great deal . . . to myself, to my homeland, even to an axe-wielding comrade I called friend. Now here I stand, bartering with the sort of miserable Rahi waste I used to hunt down."

"You have problems, I have problems," Hakann replied, bored. "We all have problems. Mine is named Zaktan."

"He controls the zamor spheres," Brutaka said. "Powerful tools in the right hands . . . powerful weapons in the wrong ones. They are the currency he has used to buy my services, Piraka. As long as the spheres are his, I won't oppose him."

That last sentence was said slowly and deliberately, leaving no doubt in Hakann's mind that he was being offered a bargain. Wrest control of the vat and the spheres from Zaktan, and this Brutaka would switch sides. That would mean the end of the major obstacle between Hakann and sole possession of the Mask of Life.

Hard as it might be to believe, the Piraka's fierce smile grew broader.

"Then we have a deal," said Tahu Nuva.

Garan nodded. "It seems we have no choice. How do you suggest we strike at the Piraka?"

"Simple," said Lewa Nuva. "They are out track-hunting for us. So while they are scattered and searching, we attack their base and take back our Toa masks."

"What if they're leading us into a trap?" protested Dalu.

"I'm trusting you to make sure that doesn't happen," Garan replied. "Let's go. The Piraka stronghold is a long journey from here, and there is no telling what we might face along the way."

Avak and Thok's search for the Toa Nuva had brought them south of the volcano, into the mysterious green belt that lined the coast. Here trees, grass, and flowering plants grew, seemingly unaffected by the drought that afflicted the rest of Voya Nui.

"There's one thing I don't understand," said Avak.

"Only one?"

"If there's so little fresh water here, and everything is bone-dry, how does this area stay so lush and fertile? If there were underground streams, I would have thought the little Matoran creeps would have found them by now."

"Remind me, how have you survived all

these years?" answered Thok. "Think, Avak, think. Why are we here?"

"To steal the Mask of Life."

"Correct. And what are we surrounded with now? What shouldn't be present but is, somehow?"

Avak stopped walking and looked around. Comprehension suddenly dawned on his face. "Life. We're surrounded by life."

"Exactly. Think there might be some kind of connection?"

Lightning flashed overhead. If it had struck Avak, it could not have done so with as much force as the thunderbolt of realization hitting him now. "Of course there is," he said. "There has to be. And that means . . . maybe . . ."

"Zaktan is betraying us," Thok finished for him. "He has us and our enslaved Matoran focused completely on the volcano, night and day, when all the while the Mask of Life is somewhere along the coast. Its power is radiating up and bringing life to this region."

"He knows it's here," said Avak, growing angrier by the moment. "While we're breaking our backs watching the Matoran work, he can sweep in and steal it away! Thok, I think it's time we had a talk with Zaktan. Let's head back to the stronghold."

Thok watched Avak turn and stalk away through the forest. "Go ahead. I'll be behind you," he said. Then, smiling, he added softly, "Far, far behind you."

SEVEN

Hahli looked around at her five friends, now both familiar and unfamiliar at the same time. Each had been given a new mask by Karzahni in place of the ones they had surrendered. Kongu had been quick enough to ditch the one he was handed and put on the Kanohi Suletu the party had been carrying. The rest were stuck with what they were given, and chose not to ask to whom the masks had once belonged.

Karzahni beamed at them like a proud crafter seeing his creation for the first time. "Far better. Who you once were does not matter, you see . . . now you are here, and so you become whoever I want you to be."

Jaller said nothing, just stared at the ground, a grim expression on his face. Kongu, too, was silent. He had attempted to run away earlier. His punishment had been to see what would have happened had he continued to defy the Dark Hunters on Metru Nui a thousand years before. Multiple abrupt changes in the flow of a transport chute could do very interesting things to a Matoran body, as he discovered to his distress.

"So what now?" asked Nuparu. "Lock us up? Kill us? Turn us into one of these empty-shell Matoran you have walking around?"

"These 'empty shells' have been with me for over a thousand centuries, toiling away for the day ones like you would return," Karzahni replied, so softly he could barely be heard. "Now you are here and, no doubt, are but the first of many. The furnaces must be stoked, the tools made ready, and to do that I need fresh workers. You will relieve them of their duties and wait for the legions to come."

Hewkii smiled to himself. They would be alive, and they would have access to tools. That was all he needed to know. Put a hammer or a chisel in his hands and he would fight his way out of this place in no time.

"You will go and tend the fires now. All

except this one," Karzahni said, pointing to Hahli. "I heard you call yourself a Chronicler. You are a keeper of histories?"

"Yes," the Ga-Matoran responded. "I record the triumphs of the Toa Nuva."

"Toa . . . Nuva?" Karzahni said, a trace of wonder in his voice. "All these new terms . . . the world outside must have changed much since I came here. You will remain with me and teach me about the new world, so that I may more efficiently expand my realm."

"I would tell you where you can go, but I think we are already there," Hahli shot back in reply. "I stay with my friends."

Karzahni shook his head sadly. "Such spirit — it will be a shame to snap it like a twig. I could show you horrors, Matoran, that would render you a mindless, screaming hulk. Will your friends show you the same loyalty when you are a gibbering lunatic, or will they turn away in disgust? It might be interesting to find out."

"Don't, Hahli," said Hewkii. "Your sacrifice won't help anyone. We'll be all right."

Hahli looked at Jaller. The Ta-Matoran nodded.

"All right, then," said the Chronicler. "I'll teach you more than you want to know, Karzahni. I'll explain to you exactly how this kingdom of yours will be brought to ruin the instant the Toa arrive, and I hope you choke on the knowledge."

The hours crawled by. The five Matoran had been tending the giant furnace, a furnace so huge that it made Metru Nui's legendary one seem puny in comparison. They had expected the former laborers at the site to drift away once they were relieved, but instead they sat on rocks and watched the newcomers with the barest flickers of interest.

"At least the fire's hot," said Hewkii. "Something works the way it should around here."

"What . . . what do you think he needs this thing for?" asked Matoro. "Do you think it's for —"

"No," said Jaller, cutting him off. "I don't."

Kongu looked around. "Hey, where's Nuparu? Did anyone see him wander off?"

"Does anyone ever?" asked Hewkii. "But he should know better than to look for things to tinker with around here. The tools might bite his hand off or something."

"Guys!" Nuparu came running down a slope from the north. "You need to see this. Now!"

Hahli paused to take a breath. She had been talking almost nonstop since the others left, with Karzahni only occasionally interrupting with questions. She made a point of detailing the Toa Nuva's great powers and how they had triumphed over so many powerful foes. *Maybe he'll get the hint,* she thought.

"Go on," he urged. "There must be more."

"I think it's your turn," Hahli replied. "As you said, it is my job to write histories. I would like to know yours."

Karzahni gave a slight smile. "It would take most of your life span to relate all that I have experienced, Matoran. I was one of the first creations of the Great Beings, I and my brother.

I was given a land of my own to rule, and so was he. I chose to make it a place where those who had transgressed could find redemption . . . or punishment . . . or perhaps that was chosen for me?"

Hahli waited for him to continue, surprised that he seemed honestly confused.

"Sometimes I remember it one way, sometimes another," he said with a shrug. "My brother chose to name his land Artakha and make it a refuge for Matoran."

"Wait," interrupted Hahli. "There is a Matoran legend about a place called Artakha . . . a land where Matoran can be safe from all harm. Are you saying this place really exists?"

"It is as real as the rock you are sitting on," he replied. "Which, by the way, is an action you might want to rethink."

Hahli looked down to see that her legs had slowly begun transforming to stone. At the same time, the rock had begun to squirm as if taking on life. With a cry, she bolted up and ran several paces away from her former seat. After a few moments, the process reversed itself.

"A very effective way to combat laziness," said Karzahni. "Those who prefer to sit around all day unmoving as a stone . . . eventually become one."

"Then those stone statues of Matoran we saw on the way in were — ?"

"Formerly willful and disobedient Matoran," he finished for her, "now fulfilling a valuable role as examples of the consequences of such behavior."

"You're insane!"

"I prefer the term 'creative,'" Karzahni replied. "Though I suppose there is not much difference between the two in the end, is there?"

"So what did you seek-find?" asked Kongu. "A new kind of bolt driver? A really great wrench?"

"Look for yourself," answered Nuparu. He had led them into a vaulted chamber that looked as if no one but their little group had entered it in centuries. It was immediately obvious to Hewkii's eyes that this had once been a busy crafting center, though he had no clue what they might have made here. *Whatever it was, they were making a lot of it,* he thought. *Look at the size of this place!*

Nuparu had walked all the way to the back of the chamber and pulled open a sliding door. Inside were a series of long tables, with stone tablets scattered about on top of them. Piled in the corners were dust-covered pieces of armor.

The Onu-Matoran pointed to one of the tablets. "I found this. It shows a Matoran, one resembling us, being rebuilt . . . even some of the organic tissue is being replaced. And see here? When they were done, he was smaller and thinner. Then the writing on the tablet trails off — parts have even been scraped away."

He searched briefly and grabbed a second tablet. "Here! The same Matoran, only this time with tools, items that can double as weapons. Then here he is, along with hundreds of others, being transported somewhere."

"I don't get it," said Kongu. "What does this have to do with anything?"

"If I'm reading this correctly, something is

really wrong here, and has been for century upon century," Nuparu said, excitement in his voice. "Remember the legend? Matoran who were poor workers were sent here, but *why* was never explained in any of the tales. Don't you see? Karzahni wasn't supposed to imprison or punish them — he was supposed to *repair* them!"

Matoro took a closer look at the image of the Matoran carved into the tablet. "He didn't do a very good job, did he?"

"That's the point," said Nuparu. "He didn't. To compensate, he gave them weapons they could use to defend themselves. And then he adopted other methods to fix Matoran sent to him . . . and we've seen the results of that. He could have made them better, stronger, more efficient, the same way the Turaga did with us. But he chose another path."

"When the Matoran sent here never returned, they stopped being sent," said Jaller. "He's been waiting 100,000 years for Matoran who never came . . . until we showed up."

"Lucky us," muttered Kongu.

"We have to get Hahli and get out of here," said Hewkii. "When he realizes there aren't any more coming, he might decide to 'fix' us."

"Question," said Matoro. "I've never seen Matoran who looked like this. Certainly there were none on Mata Nui. Where are they?"

"Wherever he sent them so they would be out of his sight," Nuparu answered. "And wherever it is, I hope they're happy and at peace."

Garan shook his head in wonder. He had spent the last few hours talking with Onua Nuva, sharing tales of their respective lands. What the Toa of Earth had to say was quite amazing. An island called Mata Nui? Swarms of Bohrok? And even more amazing, taller, stronger Matoran who carried tools, but not weapons?

Stunning, he said to himself. *How would a Matoran survive without the kind of power we have? They would be at the mercy of every Rahi that came along! Well, I hope wherever those poor unfortunates are, they are managing to be happy. Personally, I'll take pulse bolts over a little more muscle any day. . . .*

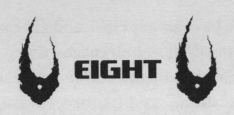 EIGHT

For the first time in anyone's memory, Zaktan screamed in pain.

Not that it made the slightest bit of difference, of course. His captor, Avak, was not inclined to be merciful. In fact, he was enjoying watching his foe's struggles.

"Keep it up," he said. "You forgot the prisons I create will work on anyone, even you. In case you wondered, you're in a resonance field. Every time you strike it, you trigger a sonic hum pitched just right to drive the protodites that make up your body straight out of their little minds."

Avak could be something of a braggart, but in this case he was telling the truth. The sound produced by the field was causing the microscopic creatures that comprised Zaktan to go insane, scattering in multiple directions and even fighting each other. With no control over his form, Zaktan could not escape, let alone strike back at Avak. It was the perfect trap.

Thok slipped inside the chamber. He had never believed Avak could do it. At best, he figured the two Piraka would batter each other into submission, leaving Thok to sweep up the pieces. One of them actually winning made things a little more challenging.

"Amazing," said Thok. "You know what this means, of course. With Zaktan imprisoned, the Piraka will need a new leader. I will accept the position with my usual modesty, naturally. A new day is about to dawn on Voya Nui!"

A ball of molten lava flashed in front of Thok's face, close enough for the intense heat to drive him backward.

"It's incredible how fast the sun can set on a new day around here," said Hakann, his weapon still smoking. "You two couldn't lead a flock of Gukko to a water hole."

Avak turned and concentrated on the perfect prison for Hakann. As he did so, the crimson

Piraka launched a succession of lava spheres. The first few missed, the last one didn't. The combination of rock and flame slammed into Avak and knocked him off his feet.

"Hakann, you idiot!" Thok raged. "If Avak loses consciousness, his prison will fade and Zaktan will be free!"

"So? I calculate it will take our former leader at least six seconds to regain complete control of his body. More than enough time for me to make sure he has no body left to control."

"You can't beat us both," Avak snarled, getting back to his feet.

Hakann stifled a yawn. "Actually, I can. But why soil my hands, when I have a new friend to take care of everything for me?"

Behind Hakann, Brutaka stepped into the light. Although confronted by two powerful Piraka, his eyes were riveted on the crystal sphere in the center of the room. Hakann had kept his promise, indirectly — Zaktan was no longer in command — and now all of these Piraka would reap the rewards for their treachery.

Gripping his massive sword tightly, Brutaka advanced into the chamber.

Tahu Nuva aimed a thin beam of fire at the lock on the rear door of the Piraka stronghold. Balta had warned that it was extremely sophisticated, and so far he had been proven right. Whatever it was made of, it was immune to his elemental energies.

"Nothing," said the Toa Nuva of Fire, frustrated. "Your turn, Kopaka."

"Wait," said Garan. "Piruk is signaling. One of the Piraka is headed this way!"

Lewa Nuva smiled. "Hide, all of you. I think I know how to get this door open."

The Toa Nuva and Voya Nui Matoran ducked out of sight, leaving Lewa standing in front of the thick metal door. Reidak appeared a few seconds later, striding down a rocky path toward the stronghold. As soon as he noticed Lewa, he stopped.

"You again," said the Piraka. "I owe you some pain, Toa."

"You owe a lot of things," countered Lewa. "Like an apology to the universe for existing."

Reidak frowned. He wasn't sure what Lewa had said, but he was pretty sure it was an insult. With a grunt, he swung a powerhouse fist at the Toa of Air. At the last moment, Lewa ducked his head out of the way and the blow landed, making a huge dent in the door.

"Very deep-impressive," said the Toa. "You will be remembered in legends as Reidak, defeater of doors."

The Piraka swung again. This time his missed blow knocked the gateway half off its hinges. Angered, he aimed a third blow at Lewa's head.

"You seem so eager to go inside," said the Toa Nuva. He ducked under the blow, caught hold of Reidak's arm, and used the Piraka's own force to propel him through the door. "Don't let me ever-stop you!"

The sound of the crash brought the other Toa Nuva and Matoran on the run. Reidak struggled to his feet, but rather than charge forward, he retreated farther into the stronghold.

"Leading us into an ambush?" asked Kopaka.

"If he's not, he'll have to hand in his villain badge," said Pohatu. "So let's try going home by another way."

The Toa Nuva of Stone slammed his foot down on the floor, collapsing it. Onua Nuva smiled and revved up his quake-breakers, rapidly digging a tunnel down below the stronghold.

"Your masks will be in the eastern section," said Piruk. "It's the most secure."

"Somehow I doubt that it's Toa-proof," said Tahu.

Reidak expected to find Zaktan in the central chamber and talk him out of some zamor spheres to use on the Toa. Instead, he walked in on Thok and Avak in battle with some giant warrior. Zaktan was nothing but a cloud of protodites swirling around inside an energy cube. Hakann was standing aside, watching the whole thing.

Reidak decided to change that. Slipping out one exit, he came in another way, sneaking up behind the crimson Piraka. He wrapped his arms around Hakann in an ash bear hug and began to squeeze.

"Let me go, you buffoon!" Hakann yelled.

"Nah," said Reidak. "I don't know what's going on here, but I'm betting you're behind it somehow. So now you're going to be in the middle of it."

With one swift motion, Reidak released his hold, grabbed on to Hakann, and hurled him toward the battle. Avak saw the incoming Piraka for only a split second before Hakann slammed into him. Thok saw the two slam into a wall, saw Avak slump to the ground, and immediately knew his night had just been ruined.

The energy cube that had imprisoned Zaktan winked out of existence. The swarm of proto-dites coalesced once more into the form of the Piraka leader . . . the very, very angry Piraka leader. He glared at Thok, muttering, "I will deal with you later. First, I have more powerful ene-mies to dispose of."

His vengeance was interrupted by a sudden crash. The eastern door flew across the chamber and smashed into a wall, crumpled like a Matoran wishing staff. Reluctantly, Zaktan turned to see the six Toa Nuva, masks restored, standing in the doorway.

"Knock knock," said Tahu.

"We heard you were trying to kill each other," said Kopaka. "We are here to offer our help in that long overdue endeavor."

Zaktan looked around at his forces. Reidak was still stunned that he had unwittingly freed the emerald-armored Piraka leader. Thok looked like he wished he was anywhere else. Hakann and Avak were back on their feet, both wondering what had just happened and how to turn it to their advantage.

"No matter our differences," Zaktan hissed, "we are still Piraka. The Mask of Life can still be ours, once we kill these Toa Nuva!"

None of the other four moved. Had Vezok been there, he would have torn into the Toa just for the sport. But these Piraka were all calculating odds and realized that, left alone, the Toa Nuva would eliminate Zaktan for them.

The Piraka leader saw what was happening and turned to Brutaka. "Help me, and the spheres are yours, to do with as you wish," he said. "I will even share their secret!"

The Toa Nuva charged, followed swiftly by the six Matoran. Zaktan dispersed his body, his best defense. Brutaka watched long enough to make sure none of the other Piraka were going to make a move. Then, swinging his blade at the Toa Nuva, he said, "Deal."

One blow . . . that was all it took. One blow delivered by some of the mightiest sinews in existence, fueled by anger and guilt and need, laid low all twelve of the heroic attackers. It happened so fast that Thok was not even sure Brutaka had moved. But the proof was strewn on the chamber floor before him in the forms of six half-dead Toa Nuva and six possibly very dead Matoran.

"The spheres," said Brutaka, looking hard at Zaktan. "Now."

*   *   *

Outside the eastern entrance to the chamber, a lone figure stood. His face was expressionless, but his eyes were those of one trapped in a nightmare. The axe he carried on his shoulder suddenly felt as if it had tripled in weight. As he watched Brutaka fell the last defenders of the light on Voya Nui, age gripped him and his spirit felt lost.

No. I can't do this, he said to himself. *I cannot just give up. Brutaka has dishonored all we stood for, but I will not let the Piraka win . . . even if it means I must join them. Before all is done here, they will learn that the Toa Nuva were not the only threat to them . . . or even the most dangerous.*

 **NINE**

Jaller and his friends were exiting the huge chamber when they heard a weak voice calling, "Wait!"

A lone Matoran staggered from a darkened alcove. First glance revealed that one of his legs was badly twisted, making it impossible for him to move quickly. His mask was badly dented and covered with rust and soot.

Nuparu rushed over to help the Matoran, gently guiding him to where the others stood. The injured being looked them over and said, "You are newcomers?"

"That's right," said Jaller. "I am guessing you have been here a while. What's your name?"

The Matoran shook his head sadly. "You know, it has been so long since anyone used it, I cannot remember. Maybe Karzahni stole it when he stole my mask. I have hidden in here for . . . too many centuries . . . and been forgotten even by my friends. That is why Karzahni never found me here, you see; no one remembers I am alive."

"We're leaving here," said Matoro. "Come with us. No one should have to spend their existence in this ruin."

"Leaving?" the Matoran laughed. "Leaving how? Can you turn invisible and slip past the Manas crabs that guard every road? Can you close your mind against the nightmares Karzahni brings? Or maybe you can soar like birds over the mountain, or fly beneath the waves in a silver canister?"

"No, we can't do that," Jaller replied. "Wait a minute — canister? Have you seen such a thing? Did they carry Toa Nuva inside? Where are they?"

The Matoran frowned. "Toa Nuva? Never heard of them. Canisters . . . canisters . . . where did that come from? Oh, yes, the canisters . . . we built them, so long ago, my friends and I. Just before they sent us here. Long and bright, they were, and strong enough to survive even a plunge into the ocean depths. We made them well."

Nuparu couldn't believe what he was hearing. "You made them? Who? Where?"

"In the world that feeds the world, of course," said the Matoran, as if shocked anyone would not know this. "The wellspring of flame that blazes bright, yet burns none but its bearer. And he, oh, he it burns until there is nothing left, not even ashes."

"Never mind the where," said Jaller, half convinced this Matoran's mind had snapped. "When did you make them, and for whom?"

The Matoran giggled. "Long before there was a you, or a you, or a you. And we made them for the destined ones, of course — we made them for Tahu and Gali, Lewa and Pohatu, Onua and cold Kopaka. In a place far, far from this blasted land, they entered the canisters, and there remain to this day."

Nuparu leaned back against the wall, stunned. The Toa were not still in those canisters. They had traveled in them to the island of Mata Nui and floated in the ocean for a thousand years before being drawn to shore. Then they emerged and set out to save the island from the power of dark Makuta. And this long-missing, half-crazed Matoran had been one of those who crafted those marvels, built to carry the saviors of Mata Nui.

"We made so many, and scattered them here, there, and in places no one would ever find them," the Matoran continued. "You never know where a Toa might need to go, you know. I still wander down to see them now and then, just to try and remember my life before this place."

Jaller did his best to contain his excitement. "Take us to see them. Please? We've, um, never seen anything like that . . . the craftsmanship . . . it must be amazing."

Hewkii, getting the idea, added, "Everything they make now falls apart in a few months. Now, crafters in your era, they knew what they were doing. Why, I bet those canisters can still travel."

The Matoran nodded. "Oh yes. Yes, yes,

yes. But you mustn't ride in them — you are not a Toa, are you? Only a Toa so mighty can ride, anyone else, woe betide. Do you like that? I made that up, what was it, 20,000 years ago. Or perhaps 20,005 . . ."

Repeating his little piece of verse, the Matoran turned and limped away, beckoning for the others to follow.

Karzahni had half dragged Hahli back to the site of the furnace. His mood, at one point almost charming, had turned foul. The Matoran he had so long held captive scattered at his approach. When he found Jaller and the others were gone, he grew so enraged, Hahli feared for her life.

"They have run," he said. The anger in his eyes was not present in his voice, which somehow made the situation all the more disturbing. "But there is nowhere to go. No one here will offer them refuge or aid . . . well, no one but the Manas. They welcome all with open claws. It's when they snap them shut again that all the problems start."

"Maybe . . . maybe they are just taking a rest somewhere," Hahli offered.

"And maybe they simply don't care about you," he replied sharply. "Look, they have attempted to escape without you. Chroniclers must not be highly valued where you come from."

Karzahni scanned the surrounding area, first with his eyes, then with his mind. When he was done, he chuckled. "Oh, so that's where they are . . . and with company, too. A fitting final resting place for your friends, among all the other useless relics."

Without another word, he marched up the slope, pulling Hahli along behind him. She mouthed a silent wish that if the others were trying to escape, they succeeded before this monster found them.

"Down here," said the Matoran, leading the group down a darkened staircase. "Mind you don't hit your heads."

Hewkii glanced up. The ceiling was a good six feet above them. They couldn't have hit their heads if they jumped. *I hope you know what you're doing, Jaller,* he thought.

"We made six," said the Matoran. "Always six."

"How come?" asked Matoro.

The Matoran turned, a look of worry on his face. "So there would not be seven, naturally. If there were seven canisters and seven Toa, then that meant the darkness had come. You don't need light if you have no darkness, true?"

Jaller wondered when the day's surprises were going to stop. An entire group of Matoran building transport canisters for Toa, and convinced that as long as they never built a seventh one, there would be no Toa of Light — it was staggering. Was this how the universe was ordered? Were destinies shaped by the hopes and fears of Matoran toiling away in some unknown chamber?

Then there was no more time for questions. The Matoran opened a vault door to reveal six Toa canisters, all resting in a row and looking almost new. Jaller half expected to see Toa emerge from them at any moment.

"Astounding," whispered Nuparu. "I saw these on Mata Nui, of course, but to see them completely intact . . . I could spend days studying these."

"You have about two minutes to figure out how they work," Jaller replied, "because we are getting Hahli back and getting out of here in them."

"No!" said the Matoran, shocked. "Only Toa can travel in these! That is who they were made for. Anyone else will die!"

"I'll take that chance," said Hewkii. "It's better than the living death of staying here."

"Let's go," said Jaller. "Nuparu, I expect you to have those things ready to run when we get back. We'll be back with Hahli."

Jaller, Matoro, Hewkii, and Kongu started up the stairs, only to stop abruptly. Karzahni was coming down the staircase, a struggling Hahli in tow.

"I believe I can save you a trip, Matoran," he said. "Two trips, actually. I return your lying friend to you, so you need not seek her out. And now that I know these canisters are here, I will destroy them. You are here to stay."

Karzahni flung Hahli toward the others. Jaller caught her in his arms and helped her to her feet. "Lying?" he said. "I have known Hahli for centuries. She does not lie."

"Then you are a liar as well, or a fool," replied Karzahni. "A great, sleeping spirit? An evil, armored shape-shifter? Six heroes who bathe in silver liquid and emerge with new power and new masks?" He laughed bitterly. "Am I some cowardly Rahi, to be frightened by Matoran fables? There is no Mata Nui, no Makuta, no Toa. There is Karzahni, and Artakha, and a universe that exists to serve our whims."

Jaller's mind raced. Physically, seven Matoran, one possibly insane, were no match for this foe. No threat of retribution from Mata Nui would work, either, since Karzahni did not believe anyone wielded greater power than he. But they could not just surrender. He would destroy the canisters and with them the best chance to escape. It was more than just their lives at stake, for he remained convinced the Toa Nuva were in deadly danger somewhere.

It was Matoro who stepped forward to stare up at Karzahni. "I was afraid on the way here," he said quietly. "Almost too afraid to go on. If it had been possible, I would have turned and fled back to Metru Nui and let the universe collapse around me."

The Ko-Matoran swallowed hard and forced himself to keep talking. "When we met you, I thought this was it, this was the reason behind my fear. You would torture or destroy us and we couldn't stop you. You could make us see terrors that were more frightening than anything imaginable, because they could so easily be real."

"Make your point, Matoran," Karzahni answered, "before I show you a vision of pain unending."

Matoro planted his feet and stared up into Karzahni's ebony eyes. "Then do it."

The other Matoran turned to look at Matoro. Why was he challenging this being to invade their minds again? Why was he inviting certain defeat? Jaller started to pull Matoro back, but the Ko-Matoran pushed his arm away. His attention was riveted on Karzahni.

"Do it," Matoro repeated. "Pluck the worst possible future out of our heads and make us live every moment of it. Prove your power is something other than those 'Matoran fables' you make fun of. Or are you just one of those legends come to life, a lot of smoke and shadow and no substance?"

Karzahni screamed with anger. The next second, a wave of power struck the assembled Matoran. The world spun away from underneath them, and suddenly they were back in Metru Nui. The air was filled with cries of fear and grief. The light of the lone sun had been extinguished for good. The waters of the protodermis sea were rising to engulf the city, and not all of Takanuva's power could buy the Matoran even one more moment of life.

The sky shook. The stars flickered and died. The ground beneath the Coliseum cracked open and swallowed that massive building whole, and the Turaga with it. Matoran ran every which way seeking some escape, but finding none. There was nowhere in the universe to hide, because the universe itself was ceasing to be.

Mata Nui was dead.

Some would perish right away. Others would survive for a while, despite the lack of food and warmth. Citizens would huddle in Ta-Metru, trying hard to keep the fires in the forges going, until finally the ocean claimed that district as well.

A small number would man the boats and try to find a haven to the south, but everyone knew they would fail. Those who did not go mad from grief would be lost in the violent storms that gripped the sea lanes.

Back in Metru Nui, Takanuva would write the last Chronicle. It would be a memorial to the Toa Nuva, the Turaga, and the Matoran. He would inscribe it with a futile hope that it would survive the cataclysm, even though in his heart he knew it would not. At last, he sat down in the center of Po-Metru, closed his eyes, and —

The vision stopped abruptly. The Matoran were shaken, heartsick, almost traumatized . . . all except Matoro. The Ko-Matoran's eyes were on Karzahni, who looked almost as staggered and shocked as his victims.

"Mata Nui," he muttered. "A whole universe . . . ended . . . my realm lost . . . if Mata Nui dies. Such power . . . more than I ever imagined . . . such power . . ."

Matoro calculated they had only a few moments before Karzahni came to grips with the fact that there was a Great Spirit Mata Nui whose power dwarfed his own. Once he realized Mata Nui existed, but was comatose, there was no telling what might happen. The Ko-Matoran grabbed Jaller and Hahli and started running for the cylinders. The others followed.

Nuparu was frantically opening the long silver tubes and fiddling with the controls inside. "I don't know if I can make this work!" he cried. "Or where they will take us if I do."

"I'll settle for away from here," said Jaller. He turned to look at the Matoran who had led them here. "Come with us. We can help you escape."

The Matoran backed away. "No. The only escape you will find that way is death. Besides, what do I have to go home to? A land that cast me out, doomed me to spend my life here? No doubt they think me dead . . . only fitting, for they are dead to me."

"But —"

The Matoran smiled. "Do what you have to do. The vision, as horrible as it was, showed me there is still hope . . . Mata Nui is not dead yet. What we saw does not have to happen. If you can stop it, you must dare anything to do so . . . Just as I have to dare leaving my hiding place to help the Matoran here."

"Jaller, come on!" yelled Hewkii.

The Ta-Matoran turned back to find the

others in the cylinders. As he climbed into his and sealed it shut, he could see Karzahni suddenly realizing what was happening. He began to whirl his chain, preparing to tear open the cylinders and retrieve their contents.

Jaller hit the largest switch on the controls. He felt the cylinder surge forward, even as he could just barely hear the other craft moving as well. Although he had no way of knowing it, the cylinder was already boring through rock as smoothly as if it were passing through still water. In a matter of seconds, the realm of Karzahni had been left behind. It was a place Jaller would never forget, though with all his might, he would try to erase it from his mind.

Karzahni would never forget, either. The vision he had shared with the Matoran had shown him there was a vast universe beyond his borders, with a power vacuum at its head. For now, this Mata Nui was no threat to anyone. If he could seize total power before the Great Spirit awakened . . . he could give Matoran new reasons to fear.

* * *

Voya Nui was as silent as the graveyard it had become. Matoran, leeched of all will and hope by the zamor spheres, labored ceaselessly on the slopes of the volcano. The only six not yet exposed to the effects of the spheres were sealed away, awaiting Reidak's not so gentle means of questioning.

The six Toa Nuva had been given over to the custody of Brutaka, at his insistence. He knew well the threat Toa represented, and he did not trust the Piraka to handle the situation. He would wring whatever knowledge the Toa possessed — not only about the Mask of Life, but other things the Piraka need not know about — and then kill them in his own way.

For their part, the Piraka had given up on even the pretense of being a team. Zaktan, Reidak, and Vezok held on to a loose alliance, while Avak, Thok, and Hakann trailed along behind trying to think of a way to avoid being exterminated. Avak considered trying to throw another field around Zaktan, but he felt sure at least some of the Piraka leader's substance was now watching him all the time.

And so there was no one present to see six silver cylinders wash up on the ice ring, much like six others had weeks before. Only the lightning in the sky was there to greet the craft as they ground to a halt. The sky was practically ablaze with electricity, as if heralding a greater storm to come.

A bolt beyond any seen before lanced from the red star up above. Midway through its flight, it split into six forks of lightning, each crackling with energy. Like arrows shot by an expert marksman, the bolts struck the cylinders where they lay on the shore. Sparks danced along the metallic surface, the blinking lights on the sides of the craft exploding. The air was filled with smoke and steam.

Slowly, the lid of one of the cylinders began to turn. Inside had been the Matoran named Jaller, captain of the Ta-Metru Guard, hero of the Bohrok war. He had been on more adventures than almost any other Matoran, braved more dangers, dared all for the sake of his friends. But everything he was and everything he had done was nothing, compared to what was about to begin.

He crawled from the cylinder and rose to his full height. The strobe effect of the lightning made it hard to see if the others were safe. He wished that he could see more clearly where they had landed.

Thought became deed. Fire blazed forth from his palm, illuminating the area around him. He could see Matoro, Hahli, Kongu, Hewkii, and Nuparu standing on the icy beach, but not as he had known them before. They were tall, strong, clad in mighty armor, and wielding weapons that crackled with electricity. Their masks had transformed from those worn by powerless Matoran to Great Masks that rightfully belonged to their new identities.

There were no cries of shock or surprise, no exclamations of joy. None of them saw this transformation as anything other than what it was: the first step toward a dark and dangerous destiny that awaited them all.

In silence, the six new Toa extended their weapons until they touched, lightning leaping from one to the other. It surged toward the spot where all six joined, then a bolt blazed up into the sky and exploded. The blast hurled six stars into the night, powerful beacons of light that fell into orbit around the red star.

Far away from the scene of rebirth, the six Piraka looked up at the new stars that now blazed in the sky. And though none would admit it, in that moment, a chill went up their spines.